PLEASE WASH YOUR HANDS BEFORE YOU READ ME AND KEEP ME CLEAN

ATTILA THE ANGRY

by Marjorie Weinman Sharmat

illustrated by Lillian Hoban

Holiday House/New York

Text copyright © 1985 by Marjorie Weinman Sharmat
Illustrations copyright © 1985 by Lillian Hoban
All rights reserved
Printed in the United States of America
First Edition

Library of Congress Cataloging in Publication Data

Sharmat, Marjorie Weinman.
Attila the Angry.

Summary: With the help of Angry Animals Anonymous,
Attila the squirrel learns how to control his angry
behavior.
1. Children's stories, American. [1. Squirrels—
Fiction. 2. Animals—Fictions. 3. Behavior—Fiction]
I. Hoban, Lillian, ill. II. Title.
PZ7.S5299At 1985   [E]   84-15860
ISBN 0-8234-0545-1

for Fritz Melvin Sharmat,
a great guy

Everybody liked Attila Squirrel some of the time, but nobody liked him all of the time. When Attila wasn't angry, he was fine. But Attila was an angry squirrel. He got mad at small things, big things, and in-between things. He got particularly mad at other animals, dust, trees, scissors, toothpicks, and chicken pox.

"I feel awful when Attila gets angry," said his friend Logan Lion. "He puts me in such a bad mood I have to go home and sit in my closet until I feel better."

"I know what you mean," said Imelda Ape. "I have to go home and lie down and take a huge nap."

One day Logan and Imelda knocked on Attila's door. They called to him, "Don't open the door if you're having the fits today, Attila. We don't need any of your ranting and raving."

Attila flung open the door. "Desmond Squirrel is playing toss with *my* acorns and I'm furious!" he said.

"Take it easy, Attila," said Logan.

"You'd be angry if someone were playing toss with *your* acorns," said Attila. "You'd roar your head off."

"Good-by, Attila," said Logan.

"We'll be back when you settle your acorns problem," said Imelda.

Logan went home and sat in his closet until he felt better.

Imelda went home and took a huge nap to calm down.

Attila paced up and down his tree. "Now I have more things than ever to be angry about. My best friends have deserted me."

Attila stopped pacing. "I will read my newspaper and try to relax."

Attila sat down and started to read. "DO YOU HAVE A BAD TEMPER? ARE YOU ALWAYS ANGRY? COME TO A MEETING OF ANGRY ANIMALS ANONYMOUS."

"What is this?" thought Attila. "There is a club for angry animals?"

Attila rushed out to the club meeting. The meeting room was full of angry animals. Someone came up to him. "I am Angelica Squirrel," she said. "Once I was angry at everything, but now I'm calm, peaceful, and loving."

"Really?" said Attila. "How did that happen?"

"Every time I had an angry thought, I squashed it in my mind," said Angelica. "I stamped it out. I demolished it. I changed it to a pleasant thought. It was easy."

"Maybe I will try that," said Attila. "Tomorrow when I'm in the car pool going to school, I will think pleasant thoughts."

The next day in the car, Attila sat as usual between Logan and Imelda. As usual, he felt squeezed. As usual, he felt angry. "Wait," he thought. "I will squash, stamp out and demolish my angry thoughts."

Attila sat and smiled. "This is my finest hour," he thought, as Logan's tail swished up and down his face.

At school Attila smiled when Rusty Horse stepped on his toes.

"Accidents will happen, ho ho ho," said Attila. "So what if my toes are crunched, red and swollen. That's jolly fine with me. No problem."

Attila smiled when Marcy Giraffe leaned over his shoulder and copied his math. "Ordinarily cheating makes me furious, but not today. I've squashed, stamped out and demolished all my angry thoughts."

When Attila got home, he said, "Well, that ends my first horrible day of not getting angry. I don't know if I can take another day of it."

The doorbell rang. When Attila answered it, Rusty Horse was there. "I'm selling tickets to the school band concert," Rusty said.

"I don't go to band concerts," said Attila.

"Buy a ticket anyway," said Rusty.

"Is that an order?" asked Attila. "Orders make me very, very angry. I mean they used to make me angry. But now I think that orders are just, well, simply wonderful!"

"Then you'll buy a ticket?" asked Rusty.

"I'm afraid not," said Attila, "but I appreciate your kindness in asking me to buy one. Have a wonderful day!"

Attila smiled and closed the door. Then he telephoned Angelica. "I'm not sure I like being calm and peaceful," he said.

"Don't give up yet," said Angelica. "It's not good to be angry all of the time. Go take a warm, relaxing bath. A warm bath soothes away anger."

Attila filled his bathtub with warm water. Then he stepped into the water and began to soak in it.

The doorbell rang.

"I won't answer it," he thought. "This bath is so nice, I'll just stay in it and soak away my anger."

The doorbell kept ringing and ringing.

"Maybe it's important," thought Attila. "Nobody would ring a doorbell over and over and over again if it weren't important."

Attila stepped out of the tub, wrapped a towel around himself and dripped his way to the door. He opened it.

Rusty Horse was there waving his tickets.

"Changed your mind about buying a ticket?" Rusty asked. "I decided I'd let you think it over. Then you'd know you really, desperately want to buy a ticket. Possibly two or three tickets. Perhaps an entire booklet of tickets."

"Cook a meal of your favorite foods," said Angelica. "It's hard to get angry when your stomach feels full and satisfied."

"Okay," said Attila. "Come over and eat with me. I will invite my other friends, too."

Attila called Logan and Imelda. "I am preparing my favorite meal," he said. "Lemon soup with parsley, thick buttered bread, and vanilla pudding. It will be a cheery, bright and yellow meal. Nothing can make me angry while I feast on it."

When everyone was seated around his table, Attila said, "This is going to be such a calm and pleasant meal."

As Attila raised the first spoonful of soup to his mouth, the doorbell rang.

"Nuts!" said Imelda. "Just when I was about to take my first slurp of this nice lemon soup."

Attila put his spoon down. "I will answer the doorbell without getting angry," he said.

Attila opened the door. Marcy Giraffe was there. "Would you like to buy a ticket to the school band concert?" she asked.

"Do you know how many times I have been asked that question?" asked Attila.

"No," said Marcy.

"Too many times," said Attila. "And I am no longer going to squash, stamp out or demolish my angry thoughts. If you pester me again, I am going to squash, stamp out and demolish *you*!"

Marcy stepped backward.

"Why don't you pick on someone your own size!" Then she turned and ran away.

Attila slammed the door. He went back to the table. No one was eating.

"Attila," said Angelica, "it wasn't fair to get angry at Marcy. She came to your door only once."

"I suppose," said Attila. "But Rusty Horse came twice with the same question. And I've got a right to be mad about *that*." Attila paced around the table.

"Well, it's okay to get angry sometimes," said Angelica. "But you have to pick and choose. If you rant and rave at everybody and everything, you haven't picked and chosen. Think about that. So when you really should get mad, you'll know it."

"I really shouldn't have gotten mad at Marcy," said Attila. He ran out of the house and caught up with Marcy. "I'm sorry I got angry at you," he said. "I'd like you to join my friends and me for a fine meal of soup, bread and pudding."

Marcy stared at Attila. "The blazing fury has left your eyes. I guess it's safe to eat with you."

Attila and Marcy went back to the house.

Everyone sat around the table and slurped soup.

And all through the meal, Attila thought pleasant thoughts without even trying.